CHOOSE YOUR OWN PATH

BIN Weevils .COM

THE MYSTERIOUS
SILENCE OF SCRIBBLES

Other Bin Weevils books to collect:

Bin Weevils: The Official Guide

Bin Weevils Puzzle Book

Bin Weevils Joke Book

Bin Weevils: Tink and Clott's Search-and-Find Adventure

Bin Weevils Doodle Storybook: Lab's Critter Contraption

Bin Weevils Sticker Activity Book

Bin Weevils Choose Your Own Path 1:
The Great Cake Disaster

BACKWARDS BONUS!

Hold this page up to a mirror to reveal a secret code,
then enter it into the Mystery Code Machine
at Lab's Lab to unlock an exclusive nest item!

YƎT8A22A4ꓘMƧ

CHOOSE YOUR OWN PATH

BiN WeeviLs .COM

THE MYSTERIOUS SILENCE OF SCRIBBLES

Written by Mandy Archer

MACMILLAN CHILDREN'S BOOKS

First published 2012 by Macmillan Children's Books
a division of Macmillan Publishers Limited
20 New Wharf Road, London N1 9RR
Basingstoke and Oxford
Associated companies throughout the world
www.panmacmillan.com

ISBN 978-1-4472-0532-6

1 3 5 7 9 8 6 4 2

A CIP catalogue record for this book is available from
the British Library.

Printed and bound by CPI Group (UK) Ltd, Croydon CR0 4YY

'Wake up, Bin-brain!'

You reach out of bed and give your talking alarm clock a hard *thwack*. It's dawn in the Binscape, hours before the start of the daily grime.

Then you remember – you've decided to get up extra early to do the gardening – your latest crop of Orange Bubble Mushrooms are ripe and ready to harvest!

Ten minutes, three cups of Weevil Juice and two Slime Sandwiches later, and you're out in the garden behind your Bin Nest, up to your knees in muck. It's a perfect day for it, too. The sun is out, the air is breezy – what more could a Bin Weevil ask for?

After a happy morning chopping down plants and tending to your Venus Flytraps, you're just considering a shopping trip to Tab's Garden Shop when Tink and Clott screech into view.

'What a stonking sight!' yells Tink. 'So glad you're up!'

The Bin buddies leap over your garden fence, landing in a heap at your feet. When you ask what's up, Tink and Clott both start jabbering at the same time. You notice that Clott has a press card stuck in his top hat and Tink is scribbling madly in a notepad, tearing sheets off and throwing them over his shoulder.

'What's this?' you ask, bending down to pick up one of the sheets. Tink has jotted the headline 'BIN WEEVIL BUYS FLYTRAP' in shaky capital letters.

What in the Bin's name is going on?

You invite the pals into your nest for a glass of something sloshy and warm.

Tink and Clott explain that it's not a social visit – they've come to see you on official business, as rookie recruits for *Weevil Weekly* magazine!

You gulp in surprise. Surely Scribbles, the Bin's outgoing newshound, has got it covered? Not only is Scribbles the editor of *Weevil Weekly*, he's the most eagle-eyed reporter in town. He's got a nose for a scoop, an eye for a story and antennae to find his way home.

'Why don't you go to Flem Manor?' you ask. 'Scribbles will give you some tips.'

'Maybe he will, maybe he won't,' flaps Tink. 'Nobody knows – because Scribbles has gone MISSING!'

Clott's bottom lip starts to tremble.

'He hasn't been seen for days,' he moans, sniffing down the tears.

You scratch your head in surprise as your friends spill the beans about the AWOL editor. Things must be serious, concludes Tink – Scribbles even missed an exclusive invitation to cover Hem's latest sweetie-wrapper hat collection and the scoop of Gong getting pipped to the post in Hair Pin Hurdles at the Bin Olympics! Every Bin Weevil in the Binscape has been looking for him, but the ed has definitely, decidedly disappeared.

Clott takes off his top hat and rummages around inside. He pulls out a recycled lump of chewing gum, a holey sock and a conker, before handing you a scrunched-up piece of paper. It's a telegram asking you, Tink and Clott to cover all of Scribbles' interviews for next week!

'Got it this morning,' says Clott, stuffing the telegram back into his hat.

'But if Scribbles has gone missing,' you say, 'who sent this message?'

'Dunno,' replies Tink, holding up his hands.

Something weevily and wacky is going on round here!

You try and puzzle out the mystery while your pals grumble about their morning. Tink and Clott have been rushing all over the Bin trying to drum up news stories, but it seems things haven't gone to plan. Clott managed to drop his notes into Flum's Fountain when he was getting the celebrity goss from Bunty; and Tink got distracted drafting his racing report at Dirt Valley! (Instead of writing, the over-excited Bin Weevil couldn't resist going head to head with Rott on the track.) Press day is looming and the sorry pair haven't got a single story ready for the magazine.

Tink and Clott turn to you in panic – can you solve the Scribbles mystery *and* get the absent newshound back on the job?

As an avid reader of *Weevil Weekly*, you agree at once – Scribbles must be helped! The three of you sit down to brainstorm the possibilities. Could the editor be held hostage somewhere spooky by a swarm of evil weevils? You all shudder, then start racking your beetle brains for a more appealing excuse.

Suddenly you punch the air. Scribbles has always had a nose for a good story – perhaps he's lying low after writing something sensational!

Tink remembers that Scribbles was last spotted on Mulch Island, trying to dig up facts about the secret temple. Could the intrepid reporter have unearthed more than he bargained for?

You grab your backpack and some binoculars, then stick a pencil in your hat – it's time for the three of you to do some investigating of your own! For now at least, the press deadline will have to wait – Scribbles' safety is more important.

'Hold on a minute,' shouts Clott. 'What about some grub? We could be gone for a-g-e-s!'

You whip up three more Slime Sandwiches and wrap them in a dirty hankie, then lead the dash for the door.

'Righto!' you cry, expectantly. 'Where do we start?'

Tink suggests beetling down to Rum's Airport and catching the first flight to Mulch Island, but you're not so sure. Wouldn't it be better to head over to Scribbles' nest first? There could be all sorts of clues nearby just waiting to be found.

'I'm with Tink!' cries Clott, sticking his hand up in the air.

'Hmmm . . .' you frown, rubbing your chin.

Whatever you do, you've got to do it quickly – you need to save Scribbles from a fate worse than who knows what!

> If you decide to stick with your gut instincts and check
>   out Scribbles' nest, go to page 11.
> If you are ready to start sleuthing with Tink and Clott
>   on Mulch Island, go to page 32.

Flem leads you out of the mall, then points across the water to Flem Manor. As well as being in his family for years, the stately pile is also the HQ for *Weevil Weekly* magazine. It's a terribly creative place – *the* venue for weevily arts and culture.

'He's locked himself up in his office till he gets better,' Flem sniffs. 'Grime knows what will happen to the magazine in the meantime. Ach-oo!'

'Don't feel rotten,' you say reassuringly. 'Me and the Bin Boys are on the case!'

You jump into action quicker than a flea in a flying circus, determined to track down the snotty editor. It's no surprise that Scribbles would go to Flem Manor – he spends more hours in the office than at home in his nest!

You, Tink and Clott skid into the grounds of the grand house, resisting the temptation to have a quick go in the Spot the Difference marquee on the front lawn. You step into the grand hallway and catch your breath.

'Jeepers,' coos Clott. 'Sure is swanky!'

He is not wrong. This building makes your crib look like a garden shed! At the top of the staircase an imposing grandfather clock ticks away the time; at the bottom two awesome Bin Weevil sculptures wait to greet you. Candles flicker and glimmer on every wall.

'This way,' you whisper, stepping nervously across the green marble floor.

The room on the right is marked with a sign showing a shiny top hat. Your heart beats faster – you'd recognize the entrance to Scribbles' office anywhere. You bang on the door, keeping your fingers crossed that the editor will answer.

He doesn't.

'Where is he?' asks Tink, banging a bit harder.

You knock again and again.

'It's no use,' you wail. 'He's not in!'

You and your pals slump to the floor, exhausted by your day's work. With a heavy heart, you open up your rucksack and share out the Slime Sandwich picnic you packed first thing. Despite all your efforts, Scribbles has weevily disappeared!

'Let's have a rest,' you suggest, putting your head on the backpack. You don't normally snooze on the job, but a power nap might give you the inspiration you need.

Tink gives a big yawn and snuggles up beside you, quickly followed by Clott. Soon all three of you are catching a well-earned forty winks.

'Clott,' you murmur, half an hour later. 'Stop snoring, will you?'

Snore! Sn-o-re!

You lean over and nudge your pal in the ribs. You were just having an epic dream about playing the bongos on the Jam Stand at Tycoon Island. You sooooo don't want to wake up yet!

Snore! Sn-o-re!

You force your eyes open.

'Tink? Clott!'

Both your pals are lying beside you with their mouths gaping, catching flies. Not one of them, however, is making even the faintest snore.

Snore! Sn-o-re!

You shake Tink and Clott awake, then stick your ear next to the keyhole. Someone inside is making that noise! The snore is snuffly, snotty and loud. Whoever's dozing there has got to have a shocking cold. And you have a pretty good idea just who that might be . . .

You and your friends run back outside. You scrabble around the great house, jumping up at the windows until you find the editor's office.

The window is shut and the blind is down, still rattling with each passing snore. You pull the pencil out from behind your antennae and jimmy the glass open, thanking Gam for your training as an Agent for the Secret Weevil Service.

Before you know it, you, Tink and Clott have lifted the window and climbed into the newsroom.

'There he is!' you cry, spotting Scribbles curled up asleep under his desk. The sickly Bin Weevil looks a right germy state – his nose is dripping, his antennae have lost their colour and his head is hot with fever.

You lift the editor to his feet and tell him that you're taking him home.

'Thank you,' he sniffs. 'But what about the magazine? Did you get my telegram?'

'Too righty,' nods Clott.

'Leave it to us,' adds Tink. 'After our adventures today, we've got enough material to fill ten issues of *Weevil Weekly*!'

The End

'So what's the scoop?' you ask, looking over your shoulder to make sure no other Bin Weevils can earwig.

'Scribbles has picked up a germy cold,' Ink explains. 'I've never seen a Bin Weevil so bunged up! He's tried everything to shake it off. Hot toddies, bubble baths, even medicine from Lab's Lab.'

You think of the red liquid you stumbled across this morning, then nod your head in sympathy. Poor old Scribbles!

'The ed got so snotty, he decided to hole himself up in his nest until he felt better,' the poet continues. 'First he stumbled over here to send you a telegram so that the next issue of *Weevil Weekly* wouldn't be delayed. Why in the Bin's name he didn't ask me is anyone's guess!'

You, Tink and Clott gasp. Everything is falling into place!

'We've been to Scribbles' nest already,' you say, 'but it looked as though no one was in.'

'Scribbles won't answer the door until he's tip-top again,' Ink tells you. 'He's even phoned the Garden Inspector and asked her to look after his plants.'

'Aaah,' replies Clott, more than a little sheepishly. 'So that weird warbling we heard probably wasn't a monster after all.'

You can't resist a chuckle. Everyone in the Binscape knows how the Garden Inspector loves to sing opera to her flowers!

'We'd better get to work,' decides Tink.

You nod. This issue of *Weevil Weekly* won't write itself.

'Ink,' you grin. 'You're hired!'

The End

'Wait a minute, Dosh,' you say, eyeing the Mulch millionaire suspiciously. 'Are you sure about that?'

Dosh fidgets in his seat. 'It's like I said, I saw Scribbles last Friday at Tum's Diner.'

'Tum's Diner?' you reply. 'A minute ago it was Figg's Cafe!'

Dosh's jaw drops in astonishment. Your Bin-tastic reporter skills have got him totally rumbled!

'Oh, all right,' he shrugs. 'I didn't see him at Figg's or Tum's – we met in the Shopping Mall.'

You look surprised. Dosh loves to shop, but his whopping wallet is used to being flashed over on the swankier side of the Bin.

'You usually do your splurging at Tycoon Plaza,' says Tink.

Dosh huffs with embarrassment.

'If you must know,' he sighs, putting down his smoothie, 'I was there on business.'

The hassled holidaymaker explains that he'd been doing a bit of undercover market research at the Shopping Mall. The shops over there have been turning such a profit recently, Dosh decided to check out the competition and pick up a few tips.

'Just trying to earn some good honest Mulch,' he admits, flushing a cringe-worthy shade of orange.

You nod your head and promise to keep stum about Dosh's mooch through the mall. He is one decent Bin Weevil, after all.

'Where did you see Scribbles then?' asked Clott.

'He was talking to Grunt in the Shopping Mall,' replies the minted millionaire, adding, 'I can see him now – he was sneezing all over Grunt's shiny taps!'

You frown.

'Are you sure it was Scribbles?' you ask, wondering if

Dosh's dosh has finally gone to his head. 'Doesn't sound like our friendly neighbourhood editor!'

Dosh pops out his single eyeglass and peers into your face.

'I'd know my old friend anywhere,' he retorts. 'Who else in the Bin has got three-coloured antennae like that? I saw Scribbles in the mall, sneezing and sniffing like Flem in a flower garden! I even had to give him a twenty-Mulch note to blow his hooter on!'

'Poor old Scribbles,' says Clott. 'He must have picked up a germ from somewhere.'

Tink is already heading for the first plane back to Rum's Airport.

'We've got to get to the mall!' he shrieks dramatically.

'Wait up!' you yell, begging your friends to take some time out to think this through. Dosh's lead is a good one, but you can't help wondering whether the editor of *Weevil Weekly* would really let a little thing like a common cold get in his way.

> If you decide to stick with your original plan and investigate the secret temple, go to page 28.
> If you want to pursue this hot new lead straight away, go to page 84.

'Please can we go to Mulch Island?' begs Clott. 'Per-lease!'

Tink rummages in his waistcoat pocket, then pulls out a pair of dark glasses. He slides the shades on and makes for the door.

'Now I'm ready for a dose of sun, sea and sand!' he grins.

Clott guffaws excitedly. 'Bring it on!'

'Whoa there, Bin Boys,' you cry, barring their way.

You hate to be a party pooper, but you've got to stay on-task! As a member of the Secret Weevil Service, your sleuthing instincts tell you to start the investigation with the possible scene of the crime. It may not be such a glamorous location as the beach of Mulch Island, but you can't go anywhere till you've checked Scribbles' nest off the list.

'We're going over to Scribbles' place,' you announce. 'Even if he's not inside, there could be all kinds of clues lying around just waiting to be discovered!'

Soon the three of you are trooping across the Binscape towards Scribbles' nest. After two Slime Sandwich stops, a comfort break and a quick chat with Posh, you finally make out the curly pipe winding round the roof of Scribbles' residence. You scamper up the garden path and bang loudly on the front door.

'There's no answer,' you sigh, creeping round to peer through the downstairs window.

Scribbles' nest looks totally awesome inside. You spot cool ornaments on every shelf and super-snazzy Day-Glo wallpaper. The stylish ed even has a white swing seat and a wind-up robot in his front room. You whistle in quiet appreciation – this is definitely a five-star crib! The ultimate in Bin Weevil style and sophistication, the place has Scribbles' name stamped all over it. Unfortunately, it doesn't seem to feature Scribbles himself.

'Maybe he's in his Home Cinema?' suggests Clott.

You peer down the hole in the corner of the nest, but it looks dark and empty.

'Nope,' you surmise. 'Even if the ed was here earlier, he's not around now! Sorry, guys.'

You clench your fists with disappointment, then pick your way back through Scribbles' garden.

That's where you see it.

There, among the wacky and wonderful flowers, is a thin glass bottle with a cork wedged in the end. Tink and Clott peer over your shoulder.

'Must be a strange kind of seed,' coos Clott. 'Maybe it'll grow into a Pit of Mystery or a Phoenix Tree.'

'That's no seed,' you reply. 'It's a test tube from Lab's Lab!'

Tink humphs, unimpressed by Lab's littering.

'Why did he drop it on the grass?' he moans. 'Very careless.'

You hold the test tube up to the light. A strange scarlet liquid bubbles and pops inside.

'It's not litter, it's a CLUE!'

What is in the test tube? If you decide to snoop some more around Scribbles' nest, go to page 41.
If you decide to grab the tube and press on to the editor's office, go to page 68.

Your head tells you to go inside, but Tink and Clott don't care about that — they've already got stuck into a fierce game of Flip Mulch outside the castle drawbridge!

'Bags be green,' chuckles Clott, kicking off the game with an irritatingly dumb first move.

Tink counters with a suitably daft response, then another and then another. That's it! You can't resist elbowing your way in to show the boys how it should be done.

'You've got to try and get *more* counters than the other player, not less!' you groan, pulling off some expert game play. A few impressed Bin Weevils scuttle over to watch.

'Very good,' snorts a critter with a swollen red nose. 'Fancy a game? Sn-ifff!'

You recognize your old pal Flem, the Bin's foremost expert on super-stylish furniture! Flem grins, then blows his nose in the biggest bunch of tissues you've ever seen. Flem has had a cold since forever, but he never lets it get him down.

Much as you'd like to stay and play, you politely decline the offer, explaining that you need to find Scribbles.

Flem sniffs awkwardly. 'He's in his nest . . . erm . . . in bed. We were hanging out together the other afternoon and I might have passed on a teensy-weensy bug.'

'A teensy-weensy bug?' cries Tink. 'The poor Bin Weevil is more bunged up than Hem with hay fever!'

'Don't worry, Flem,' you smile. 'We'll look after Scribbles.'

You pat your rucksack confidently, then make a swift exit. With a hankie, a bunch of Slime Sandwiches and Bin Scones, you'll have Scribbles back on his feet in no time!

The End

Creeaakk!

No one speaks as the door swings open. To your utter astonishment Scribbles strolls in, grinning from ear to ear.

'Thanks to you,' he says with a cheeky smile, 'I've shaken off my bug quicker than you can say "*Weevil Weekly* is weevily wonderful"!'

Scribbles explains that he picked up a nasty germ after a visit with Flem. The infected newshound got so poorly, he couldn't wriggle out of his PJs for an entire week! Lab tried mixing up special medicines to help, but the only thing that seemed to have any effect was compulsory bed rest.

You remember the test tube on Scribbles' lawn and realize that the mad scientist must have dropped it on the way back to his 8-Ball. Suddenly your mysterious morning is not quite so mysterious!

'I want to thank you guys for everything,' adds Scribbles. 'If you hadn't answered my telegram, *Weevil Weekly* would be finished!'

You hold up the latest issue and smile proudly. You'd love to relive all the highs and lows with Scribs, but right now you need to get this baby on the presses!

One thing's for certain, however – there's going to be one monster party in the Binscape tonight!

The End

'I like a slime bath as much as the next Bin Weevil,' you insist, 'but a few dips aren't going to get Scribbles back on his feet. He needs square meals, antennae rubs and hot-water bottles. He needs *nursing*.'

Clott takes a deep breath, then puts his name forward.

'All right,' he sighs. 'I'll do it!'

You imagine your pal trying to take Scribbles' temperature and pull a face. You know he means well, but the last thing the ed needs is to put his life in Clott's hands — he'd be safer with the six-legged slime monster! He needs someone mothering, someone kind and caring who won't take no for an answer if Scribbles refuses to take his medicine. He needs someone like . . .

'Boys!' you shout. 'I've got it! Follow me.'

Before you know it, you're roaming the Mulch-strewn Tycoon Plaza. All the wealthiest Bin Weevils are there, promenading round Dosh's gold-plated statue and checking out their reflections in the swanky shop windows. You don't have to be filthy rich to fit in here, but it sure does help.

'Hello!' trills a squeakily high voice. 'Oh. What are you doing on the floor, Clott?'

You wave at Posh, Dosh's well-connected and well-heeled sister. Clott is so overwhelmed at being this close to his dream girl, he has collapsed at your feet, briefly waking up to exclaim, 'She knows my name!' before passing out again.

Tink shoots you a bewildered look.

'I don't think she'll make a good nursemaid,' he whispers. 'Posh spends too much time powdering her own nose to worry about anybody else's!'

You couldn't agree more. Posh is *the* girl to know in the Binscape if you want to win friends and influence Bin

Weevils, but if you're looking for someone to wash hankies and blow snotty noses, forget it!

'See you around, Posh!' you grin. You and Tink each grab two of Clott's feet, then drag the swooning Bin Weevil to the other side of the Plaza. You prop your mate up against the window of Hem's Hats. While Tink helps him recover from the close encounter with his favourite weevily girl, you grasp the door handle and make your way inside.

The whole thing is arranged in minutes. Hem's disappointment that you're not up for buying the toilet-roll head snood she's just designed is replaced by delight when you invite her to shut up shop and spend a few days getting Scribbles back on his feet! You, Tink and Clott escort the kind-hearted fashion queen over to the editor's nest, loaded up with blankets, scarves and extra tissues.

'Darling!' she coos, when Scribbles feebly opens his front door. 'I just lurrrve how you're working those striped pyjamas.'

Now that the editor-in-chief has been located and looked after, you're free to make sure that *Weevil Weekly* keeps churning out its jaw-dropping, page-turning news stories. It's time to dust down your notebook, sharpen your pencil and head off to Mulch Island for some serious investigating. What *is* going on at the secret temple?

'Come on, boys,' you say. 'We've got a flight to catch!'

The End

For once in his life, Tink does have a point. Scribbles' dedication to newsgathering is legendary in the Bin – the *Weevil Weekly* HQ has got to tell you more about the editor's disappearance than a gross green germ trail!

You slip inside Flem Manor, then prise open the door on the right. Tink and Clott tiptoe in behind you.

'Stay alert, Bin Boys,' you warn. 'There could be clues hiding everywhere!'

Your eyes dart across the room. At first glance, Scribbles' office looks just like it always does. Stacks of paper spill out of filing cabinets, fave covers line the walls and spilt ink lies smudged across the wooden floor. Normally this place is a hive of industry. Without Scribbles in it, the room seems quiet and rather chilly.

You start rummaging through the in-tray on the main desk.

'Hey,' shouts Clott. 'I might have found something!'

Your enthusiastic Bin Buddy holds up a rather grim used tissue.

'Not now, pal,' you say. 'This is important.'

Clott waves another tissue and then another. Soon he's picked up the whole waste-paper bin – ulch! The bin is stuffed to the top and beyond with screwed-up germy tissues. You and your friends make a quick deduction – poor old Scribbles must have caught a horrible, nose-rippling cold!

'I'm logging on!' cries Tink, hammering the keys of the editor's computer.

The screen blinks into life. Scribbles' last document appears on the home page.

KIND BIN BUDDIES **STOP** NEED YOUR HELP **STOP**

CAN YOU TAKE OVER WEEVIL WEEKLY THIS WEEK **STOP**
PLEASE COVER ALL INTERVIEWS **STOP**

'Bingo!' you shout, reading the draft of the telegram that your buddies received this morning.

You cleverly deduce that poor Scribbles is too sick to work. Luckily for him, he called on the right Bin Weevils to help! You tear a Post-it note off the editor's desk, scanning the dashed-off line that he'll be in bed until further notice.

> If you decide to check that sickly Scribbles is on the road to recovery, go to page 38.
> If you think your first priority is to keep the mag on track, go to page 61.

You, Tink and Clott scamper back through the Bin, trying hard not to spill any of the purple potion. On the way you meet lots of Bin Weevils. Everyone's talking about Scribbles' disappearance, but you can't stop to chatter – your mission is in a critical phase! Bunty, however, doesn't prove quite so easy to shake off.

'Hello, friends!' she beams, flashing you a curious smile. 'What's occurring?'

'Nothing,' you reply, tucking the test tube deeper into your pocket.

'Well not *exactly* nothing . . . oof!' counters Clott, stopping short when Tink kicks him in the shins.

You flash Clott a warning stare. Bunty is a great Bin Buddy, but she's also the 'Scape's most shameless gossip. She can sniff out a story at a hundred paces! You can tell by her lingering looks and twiddly fingers that she's already sussed that something's up.

You've only staggered a few steps before the grilling begins. By the time you reach Flum's Fountain, Bunty has fired a hundred questions already!

'Would love to chat more, but we've got to push on,' gulps Clott, trying to pick up speed.

Bunty isn't giving in just yet.

'Why don't I walk with you for a while?' she says sweetly. 'I'm sure I'm going your way.'

'No, no you're not!' you reply, pegging off in the opposite direction. Tink and Clott sprint after you, skidding through the dust at breakneck speed. You don't want to be rude, but this is an emergency. Scribbles needs help! You keep running until you get to Tink's nest.

'I think we've lost her,' you puff, promising yourself that you'll take Bunty out to tea at Tum's Diner when you see her next.

Tink dives into his nest and emerges a few moments later with the shiniest spanking new laptop computer you've ever seen! The tiptop kit has even got a cool 3D screen and a little mouse that slides out of the side.

'Not bad, eh?' he coos, tucking the item under his arm.

You'd love to stay and play, but you'll have to do it later. Instead the three of you dash on to Scribbles' nest.

'DOH, RAY, ME, FAR, SO, LA, TEEEE!'

'Oh no,' whimpers Clott. 'It's that crazy crooning again!'

You and the rattled Bin Boys are scooting up the editor's garden path when you hear the strangulated cries you'd tried to escape earlier. The shrieks, burps and raspberries get louder and louder until . . . the Garden Inspector suddenly appears!

'Don't mind me,' she trills, her daffodil hat bobbing up and down. 'I was just warming up my singing voice. These plants luurrve it when I perform opera!'

The jolly Bin Weevil explains that she is looking after Scribbles' garden until his swollen nose gets back down to its normal size.

'Terrible business,' she tuts, before heading off to harvest a row of Cat Flowers. 'A virtual prisoner in his own nest!'

You sigh with relief, then rap on Scribbles' front door. The editor isn't keen on answering, but after two hours of banging even he has to admit defeat. When he appears at his nest pipe you make a feeble effort to hide your surprise – the poorly Bin Weevil's inflated conk is a shocking sight to behold!

'Dello,' he sniffs. 'What do dou want?'

'We've brought a new potion from Lab's Lab,' you say

with more than a little excitement. 'One that comes without any free side effects!'

At first Scribbles isn't interested, but you finally win him round. As Clott points out, could the medicine really do anything worse? The journo's nose has reached epic proportions already!

You, Tink and Clott carefully pour out a spoonful of the purple goo. Scribbles holds his hooter, then manfully swallows it down.

'How do you feel?' you ask.

Scribbles takes a look in the mirror. It's early days, but his nose does seem to be looking just a wee bit trimmer. Bin-tastic!

'Better!' he beams, shaking you each by the hand.

Tink has one more surprise up his sleeve. He whips the laptop out and places it in Scribbles' hands.

'Ta-daa!' he announces. 'You can use this to work from home until your schnozz settles down.'

Scribbles' delighted face says it all. You and your pals have done the Bin proud!

The End

'Kip! Kip! KIP!'

After you've tried prodding, nudging and then shaking the Bin's snooziest dude awake, you give up. Kip is firmly in the land of nod and a few hundred Bin Weevils kicking up a stink in a departure lounge aren't going to rouse him anytime soon.

'One, two, three . . . jump!'

The crowds gasp as you leap over the top of Kip's slumbering body, landing with a splat on the other side of the Weevil Air desk. An impatient Bin Tycoon decides to copy you. A family of Bin Weevils make a jump for it next, followed by Flam, Tink and Clott. Soon everyone is queuing up to get over the blocked check-in.

'It's a shame he's asleep really,' sighs Tink. 'Kip could pretend to be counting sheep.'

Now that you've got past Kip, getting to Mulch Island is a breeze! Before you know it, you are boarding the plane and buckling up your slime-splattered seatbelts. The flight is bumpy and noisy, but that's the sort of service you expect from a ticket that costs zero Mulch!

When the plane bumps down on to the sand of Mulch Island, Flam waves you a hasty farewell.

'I'm only here for the ride,' she explains, heading off to ask the pilot if she can take a peek round the cockpit. The poor Bin Weevil gives her a weak nod – it's Flam's thirty-seventh tour this month!

As soon as the plane's exit hatch is opened, you can hear the lap of the ocean washing up and down the sand. You, Tink and Clott wander down the gangplank, taking in the exotic sights and sounds of Mulch Island. An upturned fizzy-drink can waits invitingly in the gloop, while mysterious frog-like crabs sidle through the surf. Over in the distance you can see a row of parasols spread out in front of a giant Ice Cream Machine. What a dream destination!

'Look!' cries Tink. 'There's Dosh!'

You scuttle forward – your pal is right! The super-rich Bin Tycoon is stretched out in the sun, basking on a fancy deckchair with a real Mulch cover. You notice that he's swapped his trademark monocle for a single-shaded sunglass. It was only the other day that you spotted the Bin Weevil living it up on Tycoon Island, but you figure that when you're as rich as Dosh life must be a permanent holiday.

You, Tink and Clott run straight over to talk to the millionaire. If Dosh has been on the island for a few days, he might have seen Scribbles investigating the secret temple! You bombard the holidaymaker with a barrage of questions, but he only seems to have one answer.

'Can't help!' he frowns, turning his back.

Tink and Clott run round to the other side of the Tycoon's chair. You watch proudly as they squeeze themselves into Dosh's personal space, refusing to be blanked.

'Do you mind?' he snaps.

Clott leans in with a goofy smile. 'Not at all!'

'Did Scribbles walk along the beach on his way to the secret temple?' asks Tink.

'How am I meant to remember who I saw and where?' snaps Dosh. 'I'm not Fink!'

'Come on,' you urge. 'When did you last see Scribbles?'

Dosh wriggles awkwardly on his sunbed. A strange feeling slowly starts to dawn on you . . . Perhaps the Tycoon knows more than he's letting on! When he finally realizes that you and your pesky friends aren't going to buzz off without an answer, Dosh talks like a canary.

'I didn't see Scribbles on Mulch Island, I saw him in . . .

doh!' Dosh clamps his hand over his mouth.

'Where?' you ask, reaching for your notepad.

'Um ... er ... it was at Figg's,' he gasps. 'Yes, that's it, it was at Figg's Cafe on Monday, Tuesday or maybe Wednesday. Now can you go away please? My tan isn't going to go yellow all by itself.'

> If you decide to head back to Figg's Cafe, go to page 74.
> If you think it's smarter to stay and fire more questions at Dosh, go to page 9.

'Leave it to me,' you nod, pulling your antennae up to their full height. 'Stand aside please!'

The crowd parts to let you through to Scribbles' nest door. You bang three times, then bellow through the letterbox.

'Like it or hate it, Ed?' you plead. 'Put us out of our misery!'

There's a stunned silence, then the sound of six feet scuttling down the stairs. Is it you, or did you detect a little spring in that step?

'Sn-iff!'

Scribbles steps out into the sunshine and stretches. The reporter is still looking peaky, but you can see he's ready to rove once more. His jolly green colour is even coming back!

Scribbles sticks his copy of *Weevil Weekly* under his arm, then motions to you, Tink and Clott.

'Follow me,' he says, leading you down the trail that winds round to Flum's Fountain. You fall in step behind Scribbles. The rest of the team scuttle after, joined at every turn by the multiplying mob of curious Bin Weevils.

Soon you arrive at the grounds of Flem Manor. Scribbles ushers you into the *Weevil Weekly* office and points to a desk.

'Bin-tastic work, buddies,' he grins. 'You've got a job!'

The End

'This way, lads!' you yell, leading the Bin Boys across the drawbridge into Castle Gam.

'I don't like the sound of this,' yelps Tink, his teeth chattering.

Clott doesn't say anything. He's got his face buried inside his top hat.

You stare up at the menacing stone walls and spiky grey turrets. You're feeling jittery too, but this is no time for wimping out – Scribbles needs help!

Inside the castle, the décor doesn't get much friendlier. Waxy candles flicker on the walls and CCTV cameras whirr ominously, tracking your every move.

'Ever get the feeling you're being w-watched?' gulps Clott.

Of course you're being watched. As well as being Gam's home, the castle is HQ to the Secret Weevil Service, an undercover organization of elite agents that would do anything to protect the Bin. You, Tink and Clott have served on many missions yourselves, risking life and legs to save Bin Weevils in trouble.

'Come on!' you beckon, approaching the riveted steel door that leads into the maximum security control room. If Scribbles wanted to find a place to lie low, this would have to be it.

Inside you find yourself standing in a futuristic cavern lined with wall-to-wall computers, flashing buttons and laser beams. For an old guy, Gam likes to keep ahead of secret agent technology. You creep through the Special Ops zone, scouring the joint for clues. Pretty soon a rather whopping one turns up . . .

'Hello, Agents, Scribbles and I have been expecting you.'

'SNNnniiFFF!'

You look up to see Gam himself saluting you, flanked by a rather poorly-looking Scribbles! You, Tink and Clott hare up to hug your long-lost pal, then freeze – that lurgy looks too grim to share! Scribbles is the peakiest shade of green you've ever seen.

The editor clutches his throat and tries to croak hello. Nothing comes out.

'That's one bad case of Bin flu,' whistles Tink. 'Poor chap can't even talk!'

Gam nods, explaining that Scribbles came and asked him for help.

'A reporter can't report if he can't ask questions,' says the old solider. 'When *Weevil Weekly* was put in jeopardy, Scribbles came here to hide out until he felt better.'

The sorry ed tries to agree, but ends up phlegming all over an SWS radar screen. Gam winces and carries on, revealing that it was him that sent the telegram to Tink and Clott.

'You might not be the smartest agents in the Bin,' he grins toothily, 'but you are the most enthusiastic.'

Tink and Clott nod their heads, explaining how you've already been to Mulch Island and back in search of the sickly Scribbles. Gam smiles proudly.

'I've got one more mission for you. Write up your adventures for the headline story of the next issue of the magazine.'

You, Tink and Clott don't need to be asked twice. When the presses roll, you're going to be the toast of the Bin – good work, Agents!

The End

Now that Dosh has got his fib off his chest, he's back to his usual generous, jolly self.

'Why don't I buy you folks a smoothie?' he grins. 'Or maybe a snazzy new swimsuit? The sea is extra sloshy and warm this afternoon!'

It's a tempting offer, but you have to decline. How can you chillax on the beach when Scribbles is still out there somewhere, feeling lost and fluey? You say goodbye to Dosh, then drag Tink and Clott to Mulch Island's jungle.

'Let's press on to the secret temple,' you insist. 'Scribbles wouldn't let a few germs get in the way of a decent story!'

You push through the palm trees, trying to ignore the green crabs snapping at your ankles. Swarms of strange insects flit above your head. Every one of your six legs is telling you to run away fast, but you boldly push forward. Scribbles wouldn't give up!

'Owww!' yelps Tink, tripping over something half buried in the sand. He and Clott land in a messy heap. You bend down and pick up a rather dented, sandy microphone fitted with a BWTV label. Only one newshound carries a piece of kit like this – Scribbles!

You arrive at a security barrier with a note on the front:

GONE FOR LUNCH

AUTHORIZED BIN WEEVILS ONLY

BY ORDER OF FINK

You look left and right. You're not one to break Bin rules, but this is a super-sleuthing emergency. Fink would understand.

What awaits you in the grounds of the secret temple? Turn to page 40 to find out!

Clott points to the horizon. 'That's our cue to leave!'

You don't put up a fight. It makes a ton more sense to check out what info Lab can shed on this strange singing sitch before wading in with just a couple of Bin Boys for back-up.

You thrust the test tube in your pocket, then beat a speedy retreat up Scribbles' garden path. Before the phantom raspberry warbler can grab you in its clutches, you are crossing the water towards the 8-Ball at the top of Lab's Lab.

Lab's Lab is so fascinating it makes your head hurt just to think about it. As you scuttle through its corridors you pass flaming Bunsen burners, bleeping computer screens and mysterious computation machines working out sums at a frightening pace. You find the brainbox himself at his workstation, scribbling down a maths equation so long it needs four sheets of paper.

'Caught me enjoying some time off,' he beams politely. 'One of my hobbies is working out logic problems. Really knotty algebra is such rocketing good fun!'

You swap incredulous glances with Tink and Clott, then put the scarlet test tube on the table.

'Do you know anything about this?' you ask, explaining that you found the potion in Scribbles' garden.

Lab's chest puffs up with pride.

'This is my very latest prototype. I must have dropped it,' he declares. 'Poor old Scribbles is sick, you see. He caught such a stinking cold from Flem, he was too snotty to go to work.'

'Poor chap,' commiserates Tink. 'Never known Scribbles to miss a day's reporting.'

'When I saw him spluttering in the street outside Flum's Fountain, I decided to make Scribbles my next project. I developed a new medicine to make him better . . . and it almost worked, too!' Lab nods.

'*Almost* worked?' you ask nervously.

Lab sorrowfully leads you over to a computer monitor. With the flick of a button, a picture appears showing Scribbles with a nose that has blown up to the size of a Bin Burger.

'The medicine had an unfortunate side effect,' he confesses. 'Although it clears up runny noses, it also makes them puff out to twice their size. Scribbles was so shocked, he locked himself in his nest.'

Lab bustles over to a set of glass pipes positioned over a flame in the corner. A smoking purple liquid churns inside.

'I've worked out what the problem is,' he says, pointing at the violet goo. 'The mixture just needed a teaspoon more slime! I just need to persuade Scribbles to drink this new potion!'

You take another look at Scribbles' over-sized nose. It's going to take a whole lot of persuading to get him to drink any more of Lab's medicines. Even so, *something* has to be done to shrink that enormous conk.

You take a vial of the purple potion and promise to take it to the poorly reporter. Lab gets back to his sums.

As you leave the little island, Tink points out the shining shape of the Mystery Code Machine.

'Time for a quick detour?' he asks, pulling a secret item code out of his pocket. He explains that he found the code on the ground on the way over to your place this morning.

'Let's do it,' says Clott. 'That code might unlock an ultra-exclusive secret nest item!'

If you decide to take Lab's medicine straight back to Scribbles' nest, go to page 31.
If you can't resist ducking into the Mystery Code Machine, go to page 88.

'Save it, Tink,' you say firmly. Scribbles has got a mutated sniffer and there's a bonkers wailing Bin Weevil-scarer on the loose. This is no time to acquire cool nest accessories!

Tink shoves the secret item code back into his waistcoat pocket, then scurries after you and Clott. Soon you are racing up the path to Scribbles' nest. You bang on the door for ages, but the editor refuses to answer.

'Open up, Scribbles!' you holler through the pipe. 'We've got more medicine from Lab!'

Two more locks turn and a bolt gets shoved across.

'Give me a leg up,' you say, clambering on to the pipe that curls round Scribbles' nest. 'We can't give up that easily.'

And that's how you find yourself dropping in on Scribbles. Literally. You'd rather not have broken in through the upstairs window, but you didn't have much choice!

'Lab has been working on a new anti-cold medicine,' you explain, landing with a bump on the end of the editor's bed. 'You've got to try it!'

'Please,' chorus Tink and Clott, jumping in behind you.

You may not be pretty, but you are persistent. At last you manage to wear Scribbles down.

'OK, sn-iff!' he mutters, pulling the stopper off the purple test tube and taking a mighty gulp.

You and the Boys from the Bin wait for the potion to start working. It doesn't take long.

'Oh, bother!' cries Clott, his eyes wide as saucers. 'Scribbles' nose is getting even b-i-g-g-e-r!'

Will Scribbles' unfortunate hooter explode?
Go to page 83 to find out!

'Hurry!' frets Tink, scampering down the dirty track that winds out of your nest.

You give your crop of Orange Bubble Mushrooms one last, lingering look and then slam the garden gate, hoping that you're doing the right thing. Tink's plans have a success rate of, um . . . zero, so you can't quite believe that you're following his advice right now.

'A Mulch for your thoughts,' says Clott, flashing you a toothy grin.

You decide to keep that gem to yourself and lead the way to Rum's Airport. If you really are going to catch a flight to Mulch Island, you'd better get a move on!

'Who was it that said they'd seen Scribbles on the island, Tink?' you ask, spotting the neon lights of Tum's Diner gleaming in the distance.

'The Nest Inspector,' replies Tink. 'He mentioned it when he popped round to rate my nesterior decorating.'

That makes sense. The Nest Inspector is potty about the Binscape's premier holiday hotspot! When he's not rating Bin Weevil homes for his glossy *Best Nest* magazine, he spends every minute of his free time chillaxing on the beach at Mulch Island. He might even be there now! You scuttle forward a little faster, thinking that an interview with the Nest Inspector might turn up even more clues about Scribbles' whereabouts.

'There's Flam!' grins Clott, when you eventually skid to a stop outside the fluttering flags of Rum's Airport.

Flam gives you a joyful salute, then pulls her flying goggles over her face and starts running round in loopy circles with her arms spread wide. Flam has been a flying nut ever since she first jumped off her bed using her pillowcase as wings!

'Which island are you off to?' she beams. 'Mulch or Tycoon?'

You can't deny that it would be fun to hobnob with the filthy rich on Tycoon Island, but you've got a job to do! You ask Flam to show you to the Mulch Island check-in desk.

The Weevil Air departure lounge is packed. Bin Weevils in every shape and colour are queuing in droves to get away from it all! The lounge rumbles with the thud of feet and the throb of suitcases being dragged along. You, Tink and Clott take your place in the line, hoping that there'll be room for three little ones on the next flight.

'Why's it so busy today?' asks Clott, taking off his top hat so he can sit on it.

You tell Clott to have some patience, but after an hour of waiting even you are getting antsy.

Flam elbows her way to the front to find out what in the Bin is going on.

'There's no problem with the flights,' she puffs a few moments later. 'Kip has fallen asleep across the check-in desk!'

You follow Flam to the front. There indeed is Kip, laid flat across the Weevil Air ticket table, catching 4,000 winks. The rumble of feet you thought you heard was actually the sleepy Bin Weevil's epic snores!

Scribbles needs to be found! If you decide to step over Kip and rush on to the plane, go to page 22. If you'd rather prod Kip awake and find out what he's doing here, go to page 50.

'Let's scoot over to Scribbles' nest,' you suggest. Gam said that he'd seen the poorly editor a couple of days ago – surely he'd have ordered his bath and had it installed by now?

You, Tink and Clott pick your way back across the Binscape, safe in the knowledge that no despicable green slime monster is likely to leap out of the shadows!

'Of course, I knew it was Gam under all that snot,' snorts Clott, trying to forget the bit about crying and running in the opposite direction.

'That's lucky,' you grin. 'Cos there's another green thing running towards us right now.'

Clott's face fades to an unflattering shade of pink, then rosies up again when he realizes that you are pointing to Fab, the cheeriest Bin Weevil in the Bin.

'Tink! Clott! And you, too,' she beams. 'How fab!'

When Fab hears that Scribbles is poorly, she insists on coming with you.

Knock, knock!

It takes a long time for the bunged-up Bin Weevil to open his door. Scribbles explains that after his embarrassing snot-fest at Castle Gam, he decided to lie low for a while.

'Now I've had a hot bath and a good rest, I'm feeling much better!' he chirps, stretching out in his borrowed pyjamas. 'My only worry is tonight's ish of *Weevil Weekly*.'

You pull a pencil out of your hat. Tink passes you his blank notebook and you write, 'SCRIBBLES' SNOTTY SURPRISE'.

'Leave the mag with us,' you smile brightly. 'We've got a few stories up our sleeve already!'

The End

You, Tink and Clott slowly make your way out of the Shopping Mall. Not one of you can even raise a smile – you don't seem any closer to tracking down the missing Bin Weevil than you were first thing this morning!

'What's up, folks?' chirrups a chirpy voice.

It's Bunty, the chattiest bug in the Bin! Bunty is always bursting with all the latest goss. She knows EVERYTHING.

'We've lost Scribbles,' you sigh. 'Have you seen him?'

Bunty pulls her mobile from her pocket and starts texting furiously. Within thirty seconds, a message flashes up.

'Flem served Scribbles at the Shopping Mall,' she beams proudly. 'Go in and ask for yourself.'

You hold your hands up to give Bunty a round of high fives, but the gossip queen has already tootled off, babbling about a backstage pass to Tycoon TV Towers. When you step back into the Shopping Mall, Flem is already expecting you.

'Bunty said you were looking for me,' he sighs. 'SN-IFF!'

Tink and Clott nod. 'Has Scribbles been here?'

Flem sorrowfully explains that Scribbles came in to interview him for a news piece on local businesses.

'I gave him the interview he wanted,' he blubs, '. . . and something else that he didn't want. Ach-OOOOO!!'

Suddenly you realize what Flem has given Scribbles – a nose-puffing, snot-snivelling, s-t-i-n-k-ing cold! You, Tink and Clott all take a step towards the door. As the germiest critter in the Bin, Flem is Infectious with a capital 'I'!

'Where is Scribbles now?' you ask.

If you think Scribbles is at Flem Manor, go to page 5.
If you think the editor is laid up in his nest, go to page 76.

'Tink! Clott! Let's go!' you cry, leaving Scribbles to blow his nose on his brand new toilet rolls. Now that the first part of your mission has been accomplished, writing a thrilling new issue of *Weevil Weekly* magazine is going to be a walk in the Bin!

'Where shall we start?' asks Clott.

'You and Tink finish interviewing the shopkeepers for that piece on local Bin businesses,' you suggest. 'I'm going to grab the scoop of the century!'

You remind them of the recent sighting of Scribbles snooping around the secret temple on Mulch Island. If Tink and Clott can fill the inside pages, you're sure you can unearth something sensational for the headline story.

Before your pals can holler 'Bin-tastic bananas', you are on the next flight out to the island. You touch down and make your way through the gloop towards the vine-tangled jungle. Strange centipedes slither through the sand and dragonflies as big as your hand flit in and out of the trees. It's like, totally tropical!

You have to do some serious smooth-talking to get past Fink, but you're more than up to the task. Soon you've blagged your way through the security barrier into the grounds of Mulch Island's remote secret temple.

'No wonder Scribbles came here for a story,' you whisper. 'This place is the stuff that legends are made of!'

It is, too. Hidden among the palms you discover crumbling altars, carved sculptures and an ancient Bin Weevil fountain. Spooky!

'Greetings, Bin Buddy!'

Digg, the Bin's very own archaeologist, taps you on the shoulder. He tells you a story of a secret chamber buried deep below the surface of Mulch Island. Your eyes open wide when you hear the rumour that the chamber holds a secret object of enormous value.

'I'm all ears!' you cry, reaching for your notepad.

Digg puts down his spade, and points into the jungle shadows.

'Mulch Island's secrets are still a secret,' he replies. 'It's up to you to uncover them.'

And you do, too. It takes many quests, struggles and dates with danger, but you manage to unearth some shocking, staggering truths about the Island and indeed the future of the entire Bin! The tale is littered with crystals, puzzles and juggling Bin Pets.

You miss your print deadline for *Weevil Weekly*, of course, but you're sure Scribbles will understand. A reporter must never give up on their search for the truth, no matter how shocking it might be! As for the sensational headline you came up with? Now that's a whole new story . . .

The End

You sit Tink at the computer, then open a new blank document.

'The next issue of *Weevil Weekly* starts now,' you tell him. 'Think you can write something sensational?'

Tink gives you a delighted salute.

'You betcha!'

Clott drops the tissues like a hot potato.

'What about me?' he asks, desperate to help.

You rummage through the filing cabinets. In the third drawer down you find a digital camera. You hand it to Clott and tell him to get snapping.

'For today you're going to be the eyes of the Binscape,' you say, giving him an encouraging thumbs up. 'Your best photo will be plastered across the front page!'

Clott doesn't need asking twice. He slips the camera strap over his top hat then tears out of the room.

Now that the next edition of *Weevil Weekly* is in eager (if not *entirely* safe) hands, you rush back to Scribbles' nest. The editor still won't answer the door, but you don't give up that easily. You squeeze yourself through a gap in the upstairs window.

'Is that you, Lab?' cries a weak voice from the bedroom. 'I could really do with another dose of medicine.'

You remember the vial of scarlet liquid stowed in the front zip of your rucksack. Lab must have dropped the stuff on the front lawn!

Scribbles is tucked up in bed looking a sorry state. His eyes are bleary, his antennae are limp and his nose is dripping with phlegm. Luckily you have the perfect remedy. While Tink and Clott put the finishing touches on the magazine, you feed the editor two Slime Sandwiches sloshed down with the entire test tube of Lab's potion. You'll have Scribs back on his feet in no time – you can bet the Bin on it!

The End

You, Tink and Clott duck under the barrier, then creep into the leafy gloom. You part the jungle vines and gasp. There before you lie the crumbling ruins of the secret temple!

'Whoa!' whispers Tink. 'This is seriously cool!'

You spot a Bin Weevil in one corner exploring the entrance to an overgrown passageway. It's Digg – the Bin's famous archaeologist! You scuttle over and ask Digg if he's spotted Scribbles searching through the ruins.

'Haven't seen him,' replies Digg. 'But I have *heard* him . . .'

'Ach-oo!'

As you, Tink and Clott peer into the blackness below, another Bin Weevil sneeze echoes through the chamber. It's definitely Scribbles – now you've just got to get him out!

You decide to send down a chain of rescue Bin Weevils. You ask Tink and Clott to gently lower you into the pit.

It's a tricky job, but you make it all the way down to Scribbles. The brave newshound has accidentally landed himself in an underground chamber beneath the temple.

'After I picked up that cold, I bought some toilet rolls for my nose, then headed out here. There are secrets on this island that need to be revealed!' he explains. 'I sent the telegram so that you'd keep the magazine running while I was away. It was all going so well until I fell into this hole.'

You pull the Slime Sandwiches from your backpack and share them out. You, Tink and Clott are the heroes of the hour.

'Need some help unearthing the rest of the story?' you ask.

Scribbles nods eagerly.

'Let's get digging!'

The End

You, Tink and Clott gaze at the bubbling red potion.

'What was Lab doing here?' you wonder. 'He hardly ever comes out of his laboratory.'

The Bin's utterly mad scientist likes to keep himself busy. When he's not learning fascinating facts or trying out experiments, he's thinking up brain-busting new questions for the Daily Brain Strain. He's certainly not known for whiling away the hours taking in the sights and scents of other Bin Weevils' gardens! You're not sure what Lab has got to do with Scribbles' disappearance, but you're certain that this test tube has a part to play in the mystery.

'Let's check round the other side.'

You, Tink and Clott tiptoe through Scribbles' Death Cap Mushroom patch, hunting high and low for more clues. Apart from a very fine newly grown Coral Tree, there's nothing that you haven't seen on the editor's lawn a hundred times before.

'Doh, ray, me, far, so, la, teee!'

You and your friends jump in surprise. What in the Bin was that?

'DOH, RAY, ME, FAR, SO, LA, TEEEE!'

The bizarre singing is topped with a loud raspberry noise, so thunderous it echoes around the side of Scribbles' nest. Is there a musical Bin Pet on the loose? Has Lab created a Frankenweevil? Or could it be the editor himself with a particularly unfortunate case of bottom burps?

You and your pals creep up to Scribbles' Silly Scarecrow and duck behind it. The strangulated singing noise rings out again, followed by another battery of parping sounds.

'It . . . it sounds like a monster!' whispers Tink, clamping his eyes shut.

Clott hides his head in the scarecrow's straw jacket.

'Why don't you check it out?' he suggests. 'We'll wait here.'

You feel your heart thumping like a rollercoaster rumbling on rickety rails. Could Scribbles' kidnapper be lurking just around the corner? Your head wants to find out, but

your legs are in the mood for taking a break from this investigating lark.

'Doh, doh doh, LA, LA LAAA!'

The noise is getting deafening now, strangulated screams building to fever pitch. It's amazing that Scribbles' windows haven't shattered already!

'I don't like the sound of this,' you hiss. 'I don't like the sound of this at all!'

If you decide to stay well clear of the phantom noisemaker, go to page 29.
If you think you're brave enough to creep around the corner, go to page 55.

Much as they hate to say it, Tink and Clott know exactly what Scribbles would do in this situation – the editor-in-chief wouldn't rest until he'd got that six-legged slime monster splashed all over the front page of *Weevil Weekly*!

'Oh, help!' sobs Tink. 'We've got to go after it, haven't we?'

Clott's teeth begin to chatter. 'It's what Scribbles would want.'

You nod solemnly. A monster covered in icky green slime with a taste for terrorizing Christmas-obsessed Bin Weevils? Now that's something you don't see every day, even in the Binscape!

'To Castle Gam!' you declare.

The three of you tear off towards the castle as fast as your legs can carry you. As you approach the menacing fortress, you slow down to an enthusiastic trot. Then you walk a little. By the time you reach the building's rocky base you're tiptoeing like Bunty at a Bin Weevil dinner-and-dance! You decide to take a moment to summon the courage to climb up to the castle drawbridge.

'Er, Tink?' whispers Clott, forty-five minutes later. 'Shouldn't we be checking out that monster by now?'

Clott's courage is just the jolt you need. You give yourself a slap round the chops, take ten deep breaths and step up towards the castle. To your enormous relief, everything looks just like it always has done – the brooding clouds, jagged stone battlements and cracked brown earth.

'Come on,' you smile. 'Let's have a quick game of Konnect Mulch.'

It is at that precise moment that you realize what a dire mistake you've just made. You bound over a stone brick and suddenly the great green slime monster is there, flying through the air towards you.

'Aaaagggghhhhhhh!!'

You, Tink and Clott all yell back at the top of your lungs. The monster is even more horrible than Bing described! It's got wobbly teeth, bleary eyes and a weird, creaky growl. You toss your notebook over your shoulder, ditch your pencil and make a run for the castle drawbridge. To heck with roving reporting, you've roved enough!

'Yikes!'

You bolt towards the stone archway that leads across the castle, but somehow the beastie has made it there before you! Petrified, you, Tink and Clott huddle on the floor, helpless and defeated.

'Oh, poo!' wails Clott. 'Now I'm going to get eaten by a slime monster. This is turning into a really rotten afternoon!'

'At least we tried,' says Tink. 'Scribbles would have been proud.'

You close your eyes and get ready to be munched by the fiercest monster ever to prowl the Binscape.

'What are you lot doing 'ere?'

You open your eyes in disbelief. The six-legged slime monster is talking! The foul creature staggers dangerously close, then wipes a handful of gunk out of its eyes. Suddenly the fiend of Castle Gam isn't looking quite so fiendish after all.

'Aren't you going to say anything, then?' demands the monster. 'It's me, Gam!'

The oldest Bin Weevil in the Bin shakes a tub more slime off his back, then lifts his soldier's helmet in greeting.

'Why are you covered in goo?' you ask, rather rudely, before adding a hurried 'Hello'.

'Someone's been messing with the Slime Spoon Catapults again,' grimaces Gam. 'I climbed up one to try and fix it when some pesky youngster decided to bounce on that rock over there. Found myself being catapulted across the mud with only a puddle of slime to break my fall! I asked Bing for help, but he just ran off crying like a baby. Strange! What are you doing here anyway?'

You tell the old-timer all about your quest for Scribbles – from your Binscape dash through to the mysterious telegram.

'Why didn't anybody come and ask me?' he marvels. 'I saw Scribbles just the other day!'

'You did?' gulps Tink.

Gam gives a hearty laugh, then tells you how the newshound came over on the sniff for a new story. Apparently, Scribbles had a stinking cold and was sneezing all over the joint!

'When he asked to borrow a hankie, I sent him back to his nest,' grins the old soldier. 'I told him straight – I've got enough snot swilling around in me dungeons, I don't need you to add any more. Told him to stay indoors and hide his germs under the duvet! Funnily enough, I haven't heard from him since . . .'

You, Tink and Clott high five – the six-legged slime monster has just solved the mysterious silence of Scribbles! You grab your Slime Sandwiches out of the backpack and shake out the old hankie you used to wrap them up.

'Come on,' you say. 'Let's go and give this to Scribbles!'

 The End

Your head aches, your voice is hoarse and your fingers are inky, but it's been worth every hassled minute – you are finally holding a brand new ish of *Weevil Weekly* in your mitts!

And a darn good one it is, too. You, Tink and Clott watch in amazement as copies fly off the shelves! All over the 'Scape, news-hungry Bin Weevils are lining up to flick through the latest news, reviews and sport.

'Excellent work, buddies!' you declare, leading your team off to celebrate. You ought to go to bed, but you can't resist partying with your pals over at Club Fling. It's hard to take it easy when you're the toast of the Bin!

'Great party!' coos Clott, a little while later.

You have to agree with him. Inside Club Fling the crowds are jumping and the music's pumping. The lights on the chequered dance floor flit and fade in time with the banging tunes that DJ Slam is spinning in your honour. Disco dude Fling even steps out in a sharp new suit to perform an extra-special dance routine! Impressed Bin Weevils have been buying you

smoothies all night and queuing up to shake your hands.

'I could get used to this,' says Tink, flashing you a proud smile. Your pal might have landed himself a reputation for cooking up hare-brained schemes, but this time the Bin Boy did good.

You party with your friends till the small hours, only scuttling off to bed when the morning sun starts to peep over the Bin.

'What a smashing day,' you yawn, tucking yourself up in your nest. 'Scribbles must be so chuffed he asked us to help him out.'

Eek!

You sit bolt upright in bed. In all the thrills and spills of the day before, you've only forgotten to deliver the new ish of *Weevil Weekly* to its editor! You groan with embarrassment and pull the pillow over your face. You can't expect a Bin Weevil to get *everything* right, can you?

The End

'K-i-ip!' you bellow, rolling the weary Bin Weevil off the check-in desk and on to the floor. 'What are you doing out of bed at this time of day?'

Flam gives Kip a rousing shake, but he simply turns over and starts snoring even more loudly!

'Tink! Clott!' you call. 'Give us a hand! Kip's practically hibernating over here. We're going to need to rock him even harder.'

You look for your pals above the sea of antennae squashed into the airport. The Bin Boys start edging towards you, banging into suitcases and tripping over feet. You feel a tingle of nerves as the whole crowd starts to move forward too, a surging mass of Bin Weevils getting faster . . .

. . . and faster . . .

. . . and *faster* . . .

Until . . . STAMPEDE!

'Quick, Flam!' you screech, covering your ears. 'Duck!'

Rum's Airport shakes with the sound of a hundred Bin Weevils charging through the departure lounge. You and Flam lie flat on the floor, clinging on to Kip for dear life. After what seems like hours, an eerie silence falls over the hall. You slowly open one eye and squint up towards the ceiling.

'What are you doing down there, then?' Tink and Clott peer curiously back down at you, grinning like a daft pair of dung beetles.

You and Flam jump to your feet and assess the damage. Apart from one squashed Slime Sandwich and a broken lens on your binoculars, you're actually OK!

'What are we doing down here?' you rant. 'We only nearly got crushed by a marauding mob of Bin Weevils, that's all!'

Tink shrugs, before letting out a raucous cheer.

You're just about to give your pal a wallop when you

realize that he's cheering at Kip! After an excruciatingly drawn-out yawn, the blue Bin Weevil blinks and opens his eyes.

'Wh-where am I?' he mumbles, peering all around him. 'Where's Scribbles?'

'Yes!' shouts Clott. 'Where *is* Scribbles?'

Kip stretches and scratches his head.

'Last thing I knew I was snuggled up in my nest,' he says sleepily, before dropping off again.

Clott gives him a friendly nudge. 'Then what, Kip?'

'Huh?' Kip splutters awake again. 'Scribbles came over to borrow a pair of pyjamas. Don't ask me why. I fell asleep.'

'So what are you doing here?' asks Tink. 'You're at the airport!'

'The airport, eh? I'm as surprised as you are,' he sighs. 'Must have been sleepwalking again. Still, helps me get some exercise, I suppose. In fact, after all that walking, I'm feeling a bit tired now. Think I'll curl up right here . . .'

Kip slumps back down to the floor, leaving you with an even knottier mystery on your hands. Why would Scribbles want to borrow PJs? Everyone knows that he is the busiest

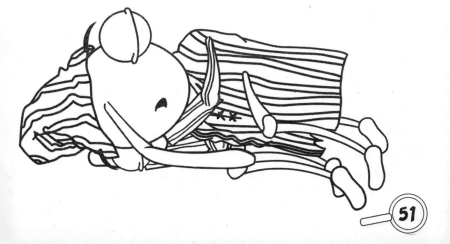

beetle in the Bin! As far as the editor is concerned, sleeping is for wimps when there is an issue of *Weevil Weekly* in the pipeline!

You try and concentrate. On one hand you have a confirmed sighting at Kip's nest, on the other a pair of rather natty blue and white pyjamas.

'One thing's for certain,' you tell your friends. 'The trip to Mulch Island is on hold till we've worked out why Scribbles has been hunting out nightwear. There are more clues out there somewhere — we've just gotta find them!'

Tink and Clott nod their heads enthusiastically.

'You coming with us, Kip?'

Kip replies with a loud raspberry of a snore. No, you conclude, Kip won't be coming with you.

> If you decide to take a detour to Kip's place, go to page 60.
> If you decide to tick Scribbles' nest off the list first, go to page 86.

You, Tink and Clott rack your brains. Where is the most chilled-out place in the Bin? Flum's Fountain, Rigg's Movie Multiplex and Dosh's Palace are all very pleasant, but they're also crammed with bustling Bin Weevils 24/7. You need somewhere tropical, with laid-back grooves and a laid-back vibe. You need the Slime Pool on Tycoon Island!

As soon as you slide down the pipe from the island helipad, you see him. Scribbles is stretched out by the Smoothie Shack, sipping on a Lime Slime.

'Dello,' he whispers hoarsely. 'Lost by boice. Ach-oo!'

'Are we relieved to see you!' cries Tink, pulling up a stool.

Three more smoothies later and Scribbles has told you all about his nasty cold and the desperate telegram he sent for help. It turns out that a trip to the Slime Pool was all he needed to help him relax and get well.

'You've been overdoing it,' pronounces Clott, helping himself to another Peach on the Beach.

'Chill out here a little while longer and you'll be right as rain again,' promises Tink.

You agree with your pals. The tropical grooves of the Jam Stand begin to play, mingling with the slimy trickle of the water slide. It really is the perfect way to unwind!

'Dank you,' says Scribbles, settling down for another sunny siesta.

You decide to join him. A tiny part of your Bin brain reminds you that the next issue of *Weevil Weekly* needs to go to press, but there's always tomorrow, isn't there?

The End

'What a rotten thing to do!' snorts Clott, shaking his head.

'I feel weevily bad about it,' sniffs Figg. 'Poor Scribbles! I told him to lock himself away till he could guarantee my customers wouldn't get nose-gunged.'

'Stinking health and safety!' tuts Tink. 'Nothing wrong with a bit of snot, is there?'

You rack your brains trying to think where a Bin Weevil would go if he wanted to lie low for a while. The answer is stinking obvious.

'Castle Gam!' you thunder. With its impenetrable walls and dark dungeons, the fortress is the perfect place to hide out from prying antennae. Tink also helpfully points out that the place is awash with snot.

Before you leave, Figg presses a parcel of Bin Scones into your mitt.

'Put these in your backpack,' she insists. 'To say sorry to Scribbles.'

You squeeze the tasty treats into your bag next to the Slime Sandwiches, licking your lips at the nosh-up you've got in store for the sickly editor-in-chief.

Soon you, Tink and Clott are skidding through the dirt towards the looming shadow of Castle Gam. As well as being home to the Secret Weevil Service the fortress is crammed with nooks, crannies, trapdoors and hidden passageways. Yikes!

If you decide to start by searching the castle grounds, go to page 13.

If you choose to cross the moat and venture inside, go to page 26.

You turn towards Scribbles' front gate, then check yourself. You think of the telegram and the ed's unexplained bailout from the job that he loves. Scribbles could be in serious trouble just a stone's throw away from you, like *now*!

'We've got to pull ourselves together,' you sigh.

Tink and Clott pick themselves up off the grass and slowly, nervously, nod their heads. One by one you step out from behind the scarecrow and stick your necks round the side of the nest.

'Morning, luvvies!'

You find yourselves face to face with the totally un-scary, un-grim and un-dangerous face of the Garden Inspector! The jolly purple Bin Weevil is wandering amongst Scribbles' plants, dousing seeds with her shiny watering can.

'Sorry about that,' says Tink. 'It's just that we heard this totally wacky noise.'

The Garden Inspector giggles modestly, before explaining that the noise came from *her*! The wacky Bin Weevil had been warming up her singing voice.

'I always perform opera when I'm gardening,' she declares. 'All flowers need music to blossom!'

The Inspector points to a lawn chair in the corner, explaining that she's been staying here for the last few nights, making sure that the plants don't get lonesome.

'What a sweet thing to do! I bet Scribbles will be mega-grateful when he sees how lush it's looking out here,' you say, before politely asking why he isn't around to do any gardening himself.

The Garden Inspector points to the reporter's nest.

'He's in there,' she reveals. 'But he's laid up in bed, the poor little bud! He's picked up the snottiest case of Bin flu I've seen in years. As soon as I heard, I came round to plant-sit. I've given Scribbles strict instructions not to come out till he's better.'

'So that's why he's not answering the door!' Clott gasps.

The Garden Inspector nods, then points at the test tube poking out of your pocket. 'You found my Venus Fly Trap fertilizer!' she exclaims. 'All 100 per cent natural!'

While she gets to work on a row of Venus Fly Traps, you have another go at enticing the editor to open his front door. That's when Tink has one of his better ideas.

'Try dangling a Slime Sandwich over the entrance pipe,' he suggests, grabbing a snack from your backpack. 'There's still one left.'

The ploy works a treat. Soon the snuffly news editor has clambered out of bed and sorrowfully ushered you inside. His nose is running, his ears are blocked and he's got a juddery case of the shivers.

'Don't worry, Scribbles,' you sigh, unwrapping the Slime Sandwich. 'We'll have you better in no time!'

With the Garden Inspector working wonders outside and you dishing out TLC inside, Scribbles really is back on his feet in a jiffy. By the next morning, he's up and ready to finish the next issue of *Weevil Weekly* all by himself!

And you? Unfortunately you, Tink and Clott aren't feeling too clever. Sn-iff!

The End

'There's no use hanging around in here,' you sigh. 'Scribbles could have gone anywhere by now!'

You quickly purchase a rather delightful new duck for your bathtub, then say farewell to Grunt. As you reappear in the Shopping Mall, Zing flashes you a dazzling smile from across the concourse. The zesty Bin Weevil is zooming around, handing out gift vouchers to wannabe shoppers. You're not sure why she's bothering – her counter has the coolest gear in the Bin!

'Let's go and say hi,' you suggest, shoving the duck in your pocket.

As always, Zing is thrilled to see you! She leads you to a gadget counter, blabbering at top speed about all the zany new merch she's got for sale. Her jaunty party hat wobbles and shakes with enthusiasm as she gets out Lava Lamps, Mobiles and Bubble Gum Dispensers and places them on the counter.

The temptation to window-shop is almost too much, but you have an important mission to see out. You politely stop Zing and explain about Scribbles' disappearance.

'Zowie,' sighs Zing, her face full of concern.

The bright and breezy shop assistant tells you that she saw the editor only hours ago – totally, utterly, miserably bunged up with cold!

'He's lost his voice too,' she adds, explaining that she sent the poorly Bin Weevil off with a free pair of clickety-clack Crazy Teeth.

'I thought they might make him smile,' she sighs.

'Where did he go?' asks Tink. 'We really need to find him.'

Zing shrugs her shoulders.

'I know zilch on that one,' she admits. 'I just told

Scribbles to relax somewhere fun. That's always the best way to take your mind off a nasty Bin bug!'

If you think Scribbles will have decided to chill out at the Slime Pool, go to page 53.
If you think the editor's more likely to be taking it easy at Club Fling, go to page 64.

'Before we go anywhere, let's get the ed tucked up in bed,' you suggest.

Tink and Clott agree at once. Not only is your statement poetic, it also makes perfect sense. Grunt gives you a grateful nod, too – if his mosaic tiling gets any more snot-splattered he is going to have to start offering discounts!

You link arms with Scribbles, leaving Tink to take the other side. Clott follows behind with the newly purchased pile of toilet rolls.

Once you get back to Scribbles' nest, you top up the generator and get the place nice and cosy. The sickly Bin Weevil is soon tucked up in bed with one of your finest Slime Sandwiches. Clott even cleverly fits a toilet roll on to a spool beside him, so Scribbles can reach up and wipe his hooter whenever the urge takes him!

You and your pals tiptoe out of the bedroom, then make your way over to the editor-in-chief's office on the ground floor of Flem Manor.

You pull up the grimy blinds, then take a seat at Scribbles' desk. Tink uses his elbow to brush the scrunched-up notes and jottings on to the floor, before handing you a spanking clean sheet of white paper. It's time to wrap up the next new issue of *Weevil Weekly*!

'What you gonna write, then?' asks Clott.

You clear your throat importantly.

'Ahem,' you reply. 'I shall call my piece, "THE MYSTERIOUS SILENCE OF SCRIBBLES".'

The End

You, Tink and Clott step over your snoring Bin Buddy and scramble out of the airport. You might just be able to get to Kip's nest and back again before the next flight to Mulch Island!

The nest is looming into sight when Bing comes tearing out of the shadows, twinkling like a Christmas tree. You, Tink and Clott do a triple take. The Bin Weevil's jaunty tinsel scarf is in a torrid tangle and his Santa hat has fallen over his eyes.

'Help!' he yells. 'I'm being chased by a six-legged swamp monster!'

'We've got to catch up with him,' you decide, making a dash after Bing's bobbing red and white hat.

Poor Bing's blinding baggy hat has got him running round in circles! When you stop the breathless beetle, he's not his sparkly, festive self at all. Bing explains that he was popping over to Kip's to deliver an early Christmas card when a terrifying green beast staggered towards him.

'It was coming out of Castle Gam! A giant, gooey thing covered in slime,' he screeches, shuddering at the memory.

Before you can ask Bing to tell you more, the worried Bin Weevil has disappeared again, vowing not to stop till he's got back to his nest and bolted the door behind him.

'I don't like the sound of this,' squeaks Tink.

You don't like the sound of it either. Your first instinct is to run, but the budding reporter in you has sniffed out the start of a sensational story.

'What would Scribbles do in a sitch like this?' you wonder.

If you're tough enough to hunt down the big green slime monster, go to page 44.
If you'd rather get on with exploring Kip's nest, go to page 80.

You gather your mates around you, then clamber on to the nearest chair.

'What are you doing up there?' wonders Clott.

You clear your throat and prepare to deliver a stirring speech. It goes something along the lines of:

'We've got to get typing, Bin Boys. The next ish of this magazine needs to be out the door, sharpish!'

The Bin Weevils clap and cheer, then bustle round the room digging out notebooks, pencils and pots of glue. You even pass round the rest of the Slime Sandwiches for extra inspiration.

'Where do we start?' you mutter, biting into your pencil by mistake.

'Everyone knows that,' shrugs Tink, wiping the slime from his chops. 'You start at the *beginning*.'

And so you do. You write down everything that has happened to you in this jaw-dropping, action-tastic, super-surprising day! A few hours later and you've written the headline story and the inside pages, too.

'It's going to be a corker!' chuckles Clott, helping Blott, the Bin's talented printer, to glue the sheets into one bumper magazine.

You nod proudly. The final

draft of *Weevil Weekly* is still a bit sticky round the edges, but you're sure it's going to fly off the shelves.

Knock, knock!

You and your friends leap up in surprise. Who could be visiting Flem Manor at this time of night? There's only five minutes before the mag needs to hit the presses. He-lp!

Who is disturbing your desperate print deadline?
Go to page 14 to find out!

'GGGrruunnt!'

Your old mate Grunt gives his usual friendly welcome when he sees you arriving. You praise yourself on making the decision to come straight here – a plumbing enthusiast like Grunt is bound to remember which fitting he supplied to Scribbles and when – a conking good clue if ever you saw one!

'Has Scribbles been in to buy a bathtub recently?' you ask. 'He would have been very bunged-up with cold.'

Grunt nods his head, then screws his face up in weevily sympathy, before comedy-coughing all over the porcelain. Although he rarely speaks a word of proper English, you are totally getting the message. Suddenly Grunt grabs his throat with both hands, choking dramatically to show you (without speaking) that Scribbles has lost his voice, too.

'We were hoping to find the ed in here,' says Tink, 'but I guess he's already scurried off to his nest to have a bath.'

Grunt nods again, then shows you all a roll-top bath.

'So he bought that one, did he?' you nod, impressed by its rusted legs and stylish slime splats. You make a note to come back for one later. The temptation to talk bathroom fittings with Grunt is nearly too much, but you can't admire taps all day! You and your Bin Buddies plunge back into the crowds milling up and down the Shopping Mall.

'Poor old Scribbles,' you sigh. 'Wish we could do something to help him feel better.'

If you decide to treat Scribbles to some extra TLC, Bin Weevil-stylee, go to page 15.

If you think the best way to revive the ailing Bin Weevil is to come armed with sweets 'n' treats, go to page 71.

'If I know Scribbles like I know Scribbles, he'll always have one ear out for a story,' you decide, trying to think where the ed may have gone to relax.

You drag Tink and Clott away from Zing's clever gadgets and gizmos, then make your way over to Club Fling.

'I don't reckon this is a good idea,' frowns Tink, gazing up at the strobe lighting and thumping speakers.

Clott shimmies along behind you, taking in the cool tunes.

'Far out!' he yells, strutting his stuff on the dance floor. When Fling boogies out to join him the vacant Bin Boy gets lost in the music, totally forgetting about his mission.

You leave Clott to strut his stuff and guide Tink to the upstairs lounge. Here the vibe is much more relaxed – a giant green sofa curves down one side, while a smoothie machine bubbles quietly in the corner. Bin Weevils lie stretched out on the carpet playing friendly games of Konnect Mulch. It's the most chilled-out venue in the Bin!

'Look!' you cry. Scribbles is snuggled up on a cosy orange cushion. The poor Bin Weevil doesn't look well at all. A reporter's notepad rests in his lap, but he hasn't written a word.

You unwrap a Slime Sandwich from your backpack, shake out the hankie wrapper and hand it over to the editor.

In a raspy voice, Scribbles explains how he sent the telegram asking for help so he could take some well-earned R&R. He then listens wide-eyed as you recount your amazing mission to discover his mystery location.

'Congratulations,' he sniffs. 'You've just come up with the next *Weevil Weekly* headline story!'

The End

You, Tink and Clott gawp open-mouthed as Ink reveals that Scribbles has fallen ill with a horrible lurgy!

'I bumped into him when he popped into the Weevil Post to send a telegram,' he shudders. 'I'd never seen such a snotty Bin Weevil! He sneezed all over my latest manuscript. And now he's locked himself in his bedroom until he's better.'

'No wonder he wouldn't open the door,' says Clott.

Ink nods. 'He's even booked the Garden Inspector to tend his flowers. Lab made some medicine for him, but nothing worked!'

You and your Bin Boys share a knowing grin. That explains the dropped scarlet test tube and the strange noises in Scribbles' back lawn! The Garden Inspector is famous for singing opera to the blooms in her care.

'The best thing we can do to help Scribbles,' you declare solemnly, 'is to get the next issue of *Weevil Weekly* on the presses. That magazine means everything to him.'

'Can I help?' Ink asks, wielding his purple quill.

You agree at once – many Bin Weevils are better than one. You send Tink and Clott out to recruit Snappy to take some pictures and Bunty to write the gossip column. Posh steps in for the society pages and Sum stumps up the business news. In just a few frantic hours, your dream team have come up with a stonkingly good magazine!

'Right!' you announce. 'Let's get printing!'

If you decide to celebrate your achievement with a well-earned boogie at Club Fling, go to page 47.
If you'd rather whisk the first copy of *Weevil Weekly* round to Scribbles' nest, go to page 72.

'So where did Scribbles go?' you ask.

Figg shakes her head sadly.

'I was too busy to notice,' she admits. 'I just told him to run off and sort out his runny nose.'

The flustered cafe owner scuttles away to take an order at another table, leaving you to work out a plan of action. Where would a bunged-up Bin Weevil go to make himself better?

'Whenever I feel rubbish, I go shopping for some new gadgets,' jabbers Tink. 'Gizmos always makes me smile! I got myself the most awesome Circus Cannon the other day. It even had a Bin Pet on top!'

You reply that a Circus Cannon is all very well, but it isn't going to stop your conk from spraying bogies when you've got a nasty cold.

'I like going to see Fab,' adds Clott. 'Her jazzy wallpapers always make me feel better.'

'That's the same thing!' you reply. 'Nest decoration won't cure a Bin bug!'

Clott looks incredulous. 'Have you *seen* Fab's new collection of Weevil Head Rugs? They're the ultimate in retail therapy! I vote we check out the Shopping Mall.'

Before you can say 'Fall in and flip out!' your mates have dragged you across the 'Scape to the bright lights of the Shopping Mall. You try to protest, but without any better ideas, you don't stand a stonking chance.

'Look through those snazzy sliding doors,' says Tink, when you're all standing outside. 'What's not to like?'

Clott nods enthusiastically. 'If I were Scribbles I would *definitely* come here.'

You shrug, wipe your feet on the mat and shuffle in.

'Wowsers!'

It's quite a sight. The mall is packed with busy critters eager to splurge! Swanky Bin Tycoons window-shop

outside Rigg's Property Shop, while budding gardeners pick out seeds in Tab's Gardening Shop. There's an eye-boggling selection of outlets, all tempting you to venture inside.

'This way!' coos Tink. 'Let's go see Zing!'

You shake your head. You love Zing's insane gizmos as much as the next Bin Weevil, but you're certain that she won't stock anything to blitz cold bugs. You stand in the middle of the mall and gaze up at the gleaming shop fronts. Could snotty Scribbles really be hiding here?

If you decide to try your luck and visit Flem to talk furniture, go to page 78.
If you think there's the sniff of a clue with Grunt and his toilets, go to page 85.

It's time to move, and move quickly. Scribbles is still lost and the next issue of *Weevil Weekly* is never going to print itself!

'Let's see what else we can find,' you shout, shoving the test tube into your backpack. 'I vote that we check out Scribbles' office next.'

'Aye aye!' chorus Tink and Clott, falling in step behind you.

You and your pals scamper towards Flem Manor – the centre of art and culture in the Bin. The grand house stands behind Slam's Party Box, its manicured gardens stretching out in all directions. It's a wordsmith's paradise – as well as being the HQ for *Weevil Weekly* magazine, the rooms of Flem Manor are packed with so many crosswords and letter grids you get a headache just thinking about it. Creative Bin Weevils stroll up and down the grounds, reciting poems and sketching potty pictures. You keep your head

down and your eyes low, hoping you'll be left to snoop unnoticed.

You are creeping past the Spot the Difference marquee on the front lawn when something rustles in the bushes. Your antennae stand bolt upright.

You, Tink and Clott split up to explore the lawns from corner to corner. You're determined not to leave a blade of grass unturned.

'I've got something!' screeches Clott, screwing up his face.

Tink scrambles over, then turns away in disgust.
'Eew!'

You run up to find a gooey trail of snot dribbling down the main path. The icky goo wobbles its way in splats and splurts out of the grounds and off towards Figg's Cafe. It's not pretty and it's certainly not pleasant, but your instincts tell you that these bogies matter. Could this be the clue you've been waiting for?

'Uh-oh,' you frown. 'I think we should follow the snot!'

Tink grimaces at the thought, arguing the case for checking out Scribbles' office first.

'The ed practically *lives* at his desk,' he reminds you.

'Let's have a quick nose inside before we go off on a wild greenie chase.'

> If you fancy the thought of poking round Scribbles' office, go to page 17.
> If you'd prefer to take your chances with the mystery snot trail, go to page 75.

'Let's split!' you grin. 'I've just had a corking idea!'

You dart out of the Shopping Mall with your pals. As you run, you can't resist sharing your cunning plan with the boys. You start with the facts – Scribbles can't work when he's poorly and when Scribbles is out of action he can't write the next must-have issue of *Weevil Weekly* magazine.

'What does a Bin Weevil with a nasty cold need?' you ask.

'Medicine?' says Tink.

Clott rubs his belly. 'Yummy stuff to eat!'

'Bingo!' you roar, escorting the Bin Weevils into Tum's Diner. 'Scribbles needs feeding up with good, healthy food.'

You step inside the restaurant and jostle for a seat. The place is packed, and why wouldn't it be? The diner is the happiest, healthiest eatery in the Binscape!

'All rightee?' asks Slum, Tum's hardworking helper.

When he hears what you're up to, Slum takes a break from flipping Bin Burgers to usher you into the kitchen.

Tum loves your plan from the minute she hears it! She agrees to dispatch regular Bin Banger, Burger and Mud Pie takeaways to Scribbles' nest in return for a review in the next 'Food Special' edition of *Weevil Weekly* magazine.

It's a double win! Scribbles will get plate-loads of healthy grub and the chance to work at home until he feels well enough to return to Flem Manor. You, Tink and Clott are also off the hook – leaving you free to play Slimeball from breakfast to bedtime! Now all you've got to do is tell the editor the good news. Way to go, Bin Weevil!

The End

You and your crack new news team wait nervously for the first copies of *Weevil Weekly* magazine to roll off the press. You've had no experience, little time and few resources to put into the project, but you're pretty sure a wee bit of Bin Weevil history has just been made. Posh's interview with Dosh is a triumph, Snappy's got a knock-out shot of Gong competing in the Cabbage Leaf Canoe Race and Sum's finance pages are bound to keep brainboxes like Lab amused for hours. When you proofread Bunty's gossip column, you got the chance to catch up on the juiciest, most tittle-tattle gossip she's ever dished. Ink has composed an ode to Scribbles and Hem's drafted the most outré piece on hat fashion ever! Tink and Clott have even scribbled a side-splitting cartoon for page 13.

As soon as the mag lands in your hot, sweaty hands, you make a beeline for Scribbles' nest.

'Come on, Team!' you cry. 'Let's go and get the verdict from the Bin Weevil in charge!'

Snappy punches the air with excitement, linking arms with Ink. 'Let's go!'

A few minutes later you're all stomping up the path to Scribbles' nest. You notice that the place is still locked up, but a gaggle of excited Bin Weevils are already starting to gather outside.

The air is filled with anxious whispers. What will he say? What if it stinks? *Weevil Weekly*'s rep could be ruined!

Tink and Clott carefully fold up a pristine copy of the magazine and post it through Scribbles' entrance pipe. You stand back and wait for the verdict.

Nothing happens for a very long time.

'This isn't very good,' gossips Bunty. 'This isn't very good at all!'

'Try to be patient,' you plead, your chest thumping like a bass drum.

After another half-hour, the crowd gets fidgety. Some fickle Bin Weevils even talk about going home.

Tink and Clott panic.

'What now?' yelps Tink. 'Dooooo something!'

If you have the courage to bang on Scribbles' front door, go to page 25.

If you are determined to stay waiting patiently in the garden, go to page 82.

You, Tink and Clott trudge back through the sand – all that effort to get to Mulch Island was for nothing! Much as you'd like to stay and whip yourself up an ice cream, you know that you daren't. You and the Bin Boys need to follow every lead that you come across, no matter how dodgy! Right now that means paying a visit to Figg's Cafe to find out whether she can dish the dirt on Scribbles' disappearing act.

Soon you're touching down again at Rum's Airport after one of the mini-est micro breaks in Bin history! You stroll over to Figg's appetizing open-air cafe. Hungry Bin Weevils perch on stools in front of the joint, snacking on Mould Mousse and irresistible Éclairs De Bin.

'La, la, la, la, la, la, LAAA!'

You hear Figg before you see her, warbling a melody while juggling four plates of Crushed Beetle Meringue. You ask the cafe owner when she last saw Scribbles.

There's a silence. Figg hangs her head in shame.

'He came in for a Bin Scone,' she blubs, 'but I sent him away!'

You gasp. Figg and Scribbles have always got on like a nest on fire – why would she bar him from her cafe?

'He had a stinking cold, see?' she says. 'Full of phlegm! I know he couldn't help it, but he was sneezing all over my customers. I felt dreadful, but what could I do? It's hard to make a living in the Binscape.'

Where did sickly Scribbles get sent? If you think Figg packed him off to Castle Gam, go to page 54.
If you think that Figg dispatched the editor to the Shopping Mall, go to page 66.

Much as you'd like to explore Scribbles' office, those yucky puddles of snot are begging to be followed.

'Take a deep sniff, lads,' you order. 'We're going this way!'

Sometimes gooey, sometimes stringy, the trail leads you out of the grounds of Flem Manor towards the welcoming canopy of Figg's Cafe.

'Anyone fancy a Dirt Doughnut?' asks Clott, rubbing his tummy and grossing you both out at the same time.

'How can you even think about food when you're stepping in and out of this green goo-fest?' wonders Tink, linking arms with his next-door neighbour and dragging him away.

Suddenly the sticky trail turns a sharp left.

'Look!' you cry. 'It's dripping into the Weevil Post!'

You and your friends run inside. The snot splats squelch up to the news-stand displaying the latest copies of *Best Nest* magazine. You notice that the *Weevil Weekly* pile of 'zines is worryingly empty.

'The trail ends here!' sighs Tink. 'I wonder who made it?'

'Not me!' remarks Ink, stepping out of the Mulch-tastic Kiosk in the corner. The Bin Weevil is the local bard, famous for his play *A Tale of Two Bits*.

Clott looks bewildered. 'So who did, then?'

Ink puts his quill to his lips, then beckons you over.

'It was Scribbles,' he whispers. 'Ssh! Keep it quiet.'

If you decide to ask Ink to take you to the missing reporter, go to page 8.

If you think it makes more sense to join forces and knock out a quick ish of *Weevil Weekly* first, go to page 65.

'I sent him home,' admits Flem. 'I knew it would hold up the new edition of *Weevil Weekly*, but what else could I do? It's more important that he gets better. Scribbles has got a nasty bug, and I should know – I've got it too!'

You can't help but feel more than a little sorry for the bunged-up Bin Weevil. Flem has been suffering with coughs and sneezes ever since he was a tiny grub!

'So was it you that sent the telegram?' you ask.

Flem nods his head.

'I faked it from Scribbles to buy him a bit of time off,' he explains. 'Then I sent him to his nest to rest up and get better.'

'Don't worry,' you smile. 'You picked the right Bin Weevils for this mission. We'll check on Scribbles, then get writing!'

'Can you do everything in time?' asks Flem hopefully, adding that the magazine is due on press in two hours.

'You betcha!' you gulp.

You've never written a whole magazine before, but how hard can it be?

Answer: writing a magazine is very, very hard.

Once you've checked on Scribbles, topped up his generator and made him a hot-water bottle, you only have an hour to get everything done! You tear back to Flem Manor and grab yourselves a blank piece of paper.

'So, boss,' says Clott. 'What's our headline?'

You chew on your pencil thoughtfully. You haven't got a stinking clue!

Tink glances up at the clock. 'Can't we just make something up?'

'Uh-uh,' you reply. 'Making stuff up is a total no-no, *but* they say truth can be stranger than fiction sometimes . . .'

Tink and Clott open their eyes wide.

'What do you mean?' they both chorus.

'I mean that all we have to do is write about our brain-boggling, belief-beggaring Bin-tastic day!'

You start scribbling so fast that smoke comes off your pencil! By the time you've jotted down the last detail, the presses are ready to roll.

Of course, the latest issue of *Weevil Weekly* is a raving bestseller. Soon everyone is talking about secret telegrams, getaway flights and missions up and down the Binscape. No one is more grateful than Scribbles – your number one fan!

The End

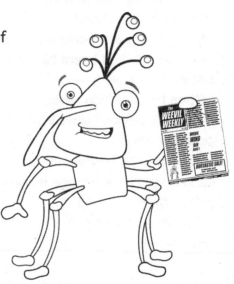

You clap your hands, then point the way to some beds on display in a window.

'If Scribbles is feeling poorly, he's going to need to lie down,' you figure. 'And this is the perfect place to do it!'

You open the door and usher Tink and Clott inside.

'Greetings!' beams Flem, scampering over to greet you. The welcoming Bin Weevil reaches out to shake hands, but then stops to blow out a humungous, nose-shuddering sneeze. 'Ach-OOOOOO!'

You mouth an apology to your pals. You'd forgotten that Flem has a cold every winter and chronic hay fever every summer! The bunged-up Bin Weevil is probably the last person to visit if you've got a nasty bug. On the counter there is a stack of used tissues stacked right up to the ceiling, stuck together by yucky snot glue. Grr-oss!

You are just backing out of the door when an object in the corner catches your eye. It is an immense Coral Bed, glowing with padded five-star luxury. The bed has its own shell headboard and a quilt to match. It also has a funny bump running right up the middle.

'Gotta check something out!' you shout, dashing through the shop. You run over to the Coral Bed and pull back the quilt.

'Scribbles!'

The editor-in-chief of *Weevil Weekly* smiles weakly up at you. The poor critter has got droopy antennae, a swollen nose and a fever that would make a Mulch Islander feel chilly. He tries to speak, but nothing comes out.

'He's lost his voice,' explains Flem, giving his patient a friendly pat.

Flem explains that Scribbles came in to buy a new bed to recover in, but was too poorly to wait for it to be delivered.

'I invited him to rest up here,' he adds. 'Bin bugs

shouldn't be sniffed at!'

Scribbles does make a sorry sight. You, Tink and Clott take a seat on the edge of the bed and tell the editor all about your mission up and down the Bin. Flem and Scribbles listen in amazement and then delight when you decide to share out the Slime Sandwiches in your backpack.

When you've finished, Scribbles' eyes light up. He points a shaky finger to the pencil tucked in your hat. Then he reaches for Clott's notepad and starts to write. Before you know it, the jaded journo has written an utterly inspired headline story for the latest edition of *Weevil Weekly*, starring . . . you!

The End

'I never signed up for six-legged slime monsters!' Clott groans. 'I thought we were meant to be looking for Scribbles.'

Tink nods his head furiously.

'First things first and all that,' he agrees. 'We haven't even checked out Kip's nest yet. Scribbles could be just round the corner! What if we scooted straight past him in our rush to get acquainted with a silly monster!'

When Tink puts it like *that*, your sensational news story doesn't sound quite so sensationally sensational.

'OK,' you shrug. 'Let's see what we can find round here. We have an hour before the next flight to Mulch Island.'

The three of you split up, deciding to search the garden first. Before you know it you are poking your way through Kip's collection of Spotted Cap mushrooms. Every few metres you spot a flattened area of grass where Kip has curled up and taken forty winks.

'Erk!' you groan, feeling your toes plunge into a particularly thorny Pit of Mystery.

'Oh great,' you mutter. 'Now I'm stuck here forev-ahhhh!'

Not only are your toes trapped – now your throat is dry and your palms are sweaty. There, standing less than an antennae-bop in front of you, is the great six-legged slime monster that Bing warned you about! You wait, speechless and terrified. Now the awful fiend has come to seek you out!

'I think Bing left his earmuffs outside my place,' says the monster by way of introduction, in a far more polite manner than you were expecting. The vile beast gently leans over and passes you a perfectly intact pair of earmuffs.

'Um, thanks,' you say, 'Mr . . . er, Monster.'

'Mr Monster?' replies the beast, incredulous.

'Oh, OK then, Sir Monster,' you quickly ad-lib, before throwing a quick 'Your Lordship' in for good measure.

It's only then that the beast reveals its most shocking tactic yet. The thing in front of you starts to scrape at its face. To your astonishment, the green slime scrapes away to reveal Gam, the oldest Bin Weevil in the Bin! As well as being the head of the Secret Weevil Service, Gam has been an active superhero since you were knee-high to a cockroach.

'Excuse the state of me, too,' he apologizes. 'Young Scribbles splattered and sneezed all over me helmet. Got a stinking cold, that one – never seen so many bogies!'

You gasp in surprise at the news that Scribbles is alive and well. Or at least alive.

'Tink! Clott!' you cry. 'Come here!'

The Boys from the Bin skid round the corner, catch sight of Gam and then try and skid away again. You manage to grab Tink's waistcoat in the nick of time.

When everyone's recovered, de-snotted and detached themselves, Gam recalls his sneezy encounter with Scribbles. The poor editor-in-chief was in such a fluey state that Gam sent him off to Grunt to buy a bathtub for his nest.

'A hot bath is the only way to cure a cold like that,' decides Gam, 'and that Bin Weevil has got the worst one I've ever sniffed. Can hardly speak a word, his voice is so hoarse.'

The old soldier gives you a friendly salute, then sets out for home.

'Poor Scribbles!' sighs Tink. 'Let's go and give the bunged-up Bin Weevil a helping hand.'

If you decide to go straight to Scribbles' nest,
    go to page 34.
If you think the smart move is to nip out and have a
    word with Grunt, go to page 63.

81

You persuade your pal to hang in there. 'That mag was packed with facts and stats,' you tell Tink. 'Scribbles needs time to take in every word.'

The crowd aren't so sure. Slowly but steadily, they drift away. 'Got to get on and do the Daily Brain Strain,' mutters one.

'Can't stand here all day,' sighs another.

Even your team are getting fidgety. Bunty has to dash to a star-spotting date at Tycoon Towers and Snappy needs to open her Photo Shop.

Before you know it, just you, Tink and Clott are standing in the shadows of Scribbles' nest. You dig the last of the Slime Sandwiches out of your backpack, but even super-smiley Clott is beginning to wobble.

'Greetings, hotshot reporters!'

Scribbles sticks his head out of his bedroom window, flashing you the most dazzling smile ever! In one hand he is clutching a notebook. In the other he's waving a pencil. It can only mean one thing – the editor is back on the job!

Scribbles scuttles down the stairs three at a time, waving the new issue of *Weevil Weekly*. He crumples up his last tissue and explains that your superb editorial work has been just the medicine he needed. After thanking you, Tink and Clott at least a dozen times, he invites you in for a celebratory cup of Weevil Juice.

'There's just one final job to do,' says Scribbles. 'I want to interview *you*. Your adventures in the Binscape are going to be headline news!'

The End

Disastro! You and your pals watch in horror as Scribbles' sore nose does indeed grow even larger.

'Oh, nooooo!' he cries, sticking his head under the covers.

'We've got to do something,' urges Tink. 'Now!'

You rack your brains in desperation.

'Lab said that the medicine needed more slime,' you jabber. 'Perhaps he still hasn't added enough?'

'Where are we going to get a splodge of slime from?' sniffs Clott.

'How about . . . *here*?' you cry, tipping your last Slime Sandwich on to Scribbles' duvet.

Although you say it yourself, it's a stroke of utter genius. After carefully squeezing the squidged sandwich filling into the test tube, you coax Scribbles into trying one last teeny teaspoonful. No one is more surprised than you when the potion actually starts to work! Scribbles' nose shrinks down to the size of a prize-winning marrow before finally pinging back into the pert green appendage you all know and love.

'I feel like a Bin Weevil again. Thank you!' he beams.

It's a stonking good end to a stonking good story. You and your pals are just discussing the best headline for *Weevil Weekly* when a troubling trill echoes up from the garden.

'Yikes!' yelps Clott, covering his eyes.

Tink's teeth start to chatter. 'It's the screech monster again!'

You peep out the window to see the Garden Inspector waving back up at you.

'Don't mind me, luvvies,' she beams. 'Just singing to Scribbles' seedlings. Plants need music! Perfect day for it, eh?'

The End

Suddenly Clott's voice echoes across the beach.

'The plane leaves in five minutes!'

The Bin Boys have made the decision for you — you're heading over to the Shopping Mall. You give Dosh a resigned wave, then scuttle along the shore crying, 'Wait for me!'

You're nearly out of time. The Weevil Air flight has started taxiing already! You puff and pant after the plane, but the boarding staircase is already being kicked into the sand.

'Grab my hand!' calls Flam, peering out of the doorway.

You grab Flam's wrist just in time.

That was too close for comfort! You recover your breath, then take yourself to a seat.

As soon as the plane touches down on the mainland, you, Tink and Clott make a dash for the Shopping Mall. There's only one place to start — you have to find Grunt! You push open the double doors and step into the showroom. Racks of gleaming toasters line up next to the latest microwaves and the coolest tiling around. Grunt takes a real pride in his merchandise. No wonder he was awarded a gold plug necklace for 'Plumbing Achievements in the Binscape'!

The shopkeeper smiles across the counter. Grunt explains that the editor came in to buy a job lot of toilet rolls. Poor Scribbles had such a rotten cold, he was sneezing through a hundred sheets an hour!

'Where is he now?' you ask.

Grunt raises his hands apologetically.

'Blow it!' groans Clott. 'We're back to square one.'

If you fancy a chat with Flem next, go to page 35.
If you decide to pick Zing's brains, go to page 57.

You scratch your head, unsure where to turn.

'SN-IFFFF!'

'Did you hear that?' you whisper to Tink and Clott. 'It's coming from inside that shop – there, beside those sinks!'

You push open the bright orange doors and tiptoe inside. There at the counter is Scribbles, handing over a wodge of Mulch! The snotty editor doesn't look at all well. He's got droopy antennae and a nose that's puffed up like a watermelon. Grunt is knelt over beside him, lifting a job lot of toilet rolls out of a slime-splattered cabinet.

'Are those rolls for you?' asks Tink, giving Scribbles a friendly slap on the back that nearly knocks him over.

Scribbles tries to reply, but nothing comes out. Instead he tears off a handful of toilet paper and gives his nose a big blow.

'Gr-unt,' sighs Grunt with his customary eloquence.

'Oh dear,' you nod. 'So Scribbles has lost his voice, too.'

Grunt somehow manages to explain that Scribbles was doing interviews with local businesses when he picked up a nasty cold from Flem. The dedicated reporter tried to keep working, but when his voice gave out he was forced to put the next issue of *Weevil Weekly* on hold.

'We got your telegram,' says Clott. 'We can help!'

Tink nods proudly. 'We'll take care of the next ish. Don't worry.'

Scribbles gives you all a grateful, but slightly nervous nod.

If you decide to find a story to save the magazine, go to page 36.
If you think a smart Bin Weevil would take Scribbles and his toilet rolls home first, go to page 59.

'Let's think this through,' you muse, doing your best Sherlock impression. 'When would a Bin Weevil get into his nightclothes?'

'When his day clothes are in the wash?' suggests Tink helpfully.

Clott has a suggestion, too. You can hardly bear it.

'That's silly,' he guffaws. 'I bet Scribbles has got an invite for a super-glam pyjama party over at Club Fling!'

Flam decides it's time to make a break for the Departures exit.

'I'll leave the puzzling to you experts,' she shrugs. 'But *I* only wear my pyjamas when I go to bed. Bye, guys!'

'Thank you!' you cry, sad to see the only sensible member of your group disappear into the sunset. 'Let's get over to Scribbles' nest like, yesterday!'

Not quite yesterday (or even this morning), but only a very few minutes later, you find yourself banging on Scribbles' front door.

'Scribbles!' yells Tink. 'Are you in there?'

'I'm dumbing!' yelps a tiny voice from inside. 'Gib me a dinute.'

'I'm dumbing?' you mouth.

There's the clanking of locks being pulled and keys being rattled. You, Tink and Clott jump back as Scribbles himself comes tumbling out of the nest's pipe slide, landing in the dirt with a *thud*.

'Dello,' he groans, his voice no more than a whisper. 'I lost by boice!'

You rub your eyes. This is Scribbles, but not as you know him. Apart from being decked out in Kip's spare PJs, the reporter's nose has swollen to the size of a small marrow! You realize that the beleaguered Bin critter has gone and got himself a stinking, snot-soaked cold!

'So that's why you've been hiding,' you cry. 'You've lost your voice!'

Scribbles hangs his head in shame. After a testing game of charades, you work out that it was him that sent the telegram asking for your help with *Weevil Weekly* magazine! The embarrassed editor-in-chief has decided to hole himself up in the nest until he is fit enough to dust down his notepad and start interviewing again.

Are you equal to the challenge of getting an issue on press while Scribbles recovers? You, Tink and Clott straighten your backs. Of course you are! Your first headline is in the bag already – 'SUPER SLEUTHS SAVE SICK SCRIBBLES!'

The End

You take a quick look at your watch. You really ought to get straight over to Scribbles' nest (that giant nose needs urgent attention!), but when Tink promises to share his mystery reward with you and Clott, the offer is too good to refuse.

The three of you bundle into the metal booth and close the door.

Tink carefully keys in the code, letter by letter. You feel yourself trembling with excitement, wondering what the prize could be.

'Go on!' urges Clott. 'Press the submit button!'

Tink hits the keyboard with a flourish, then steps back. The screen flashes and tinkles as it computes the code. Suddenly a new message appears:

CONGRATULATIONS!
YOU HAVE BEEN AWARDED A LAPTOP

You and your mates share a psyched high five. What a Bin-tastically brilliant prize! The shiny new laptop will be delivered to Tink's nest in a matter of minutes.

'Now let's get on to Scribbles' nest,' you say. 'We can pick up the computer on the way.'

Can you make Scribbles take his new medicine?
Go to page 19 to find out!